For Seung-Min and Ji-Yoon.
And thanks to the gentleman with a great big hole in his sock!

First American Edition 2014
Kane Miller, A Division of EDC Publishing

Text and illustrations © Tania Sohn, 2011

For information contact:
Kane Miller, A Division of EDC Publishing
PO Box 470663
Tulsa, OK 74147-0663
**www.kanemiller.com**
**www.edcpub.com**
**www.usbornebooksandmore.com**

Library of Congress Control Number: 2013939409

Manufactured by Regent Publishing Services, Hong Kong
Printed November 2013 in ShenZhen, Guangdong, China

ISBN: 978-1-61067-244-3

1 2 3 4 5 6 7 8 9 10

# Socks!

Tania Sohn

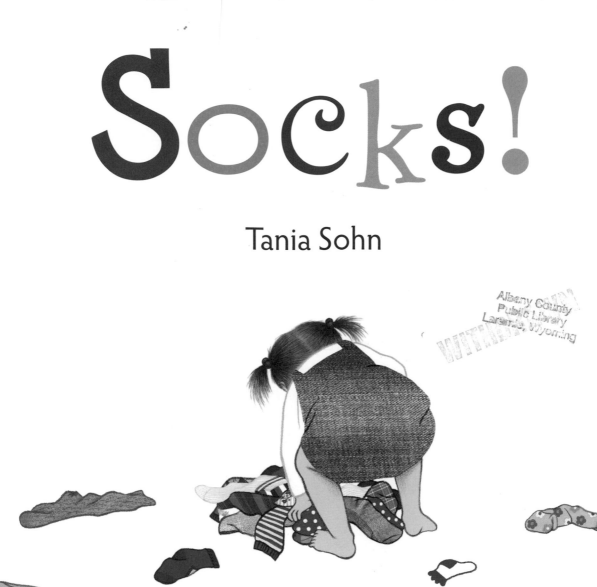

**Kane Miller**
A DIVISION OF EDC PUBLISHING

I love socks!
Socks with polka dots,

and socks with stripes.

Green socks so I can hop …

. . . and yellow socks so I can play.

Holey socks!

I love baby socks,

and daddy socks.

Christmas socks!

Ankle socks so I can fly ...

... and knee socks so I can trumpet. Aroo!

Puppet socks!

What kind of socks are these?

Beoseon! Traditional Korean socks,
from Grandma.

Polka dot socks, striped socks,
green socks, yellow socks, holey socks,
baby socks, daddy socks, Christmas socks,
ankle socks, knee socks, puppet socks,
socks from grandma ... my socks!

I love socks!

Tania Sohn earned an MA in Children's Book Illustration
from Cambridge School of Art in the United Kingdom.
She now lives and works in Seoul, Korea.
She loves socks and has quite a collection.